MW01071577

What's the Matter with Mr. Fuego?

Torrey Maloof

Publishing Credits

Corinne Burton, M.A.Ed., *President*
Conni Medina, M.A.Ed., *Managing Editor*
Diana Kenney, M.A.Ed., NBCT, *Content Director*
Emily R. Smith, M.A.Ed., *Series Developer*
Courtney Patterson, *Multimedia Designer*

Image Credits: Cover, 2–3, 7–32: Travis Hanson; all other images: Shutterstock

Library of Congress Cataloging-in-Publication Data

Maloof, Torrey, author.
  What's the matter with Mr. Fuego? / Torrey Maloof.
    pages cm
  Summary: "Mr. Fuego is a beloved science teacher at Albert Einstein Intermediate. He is known for his amazing demonstrations of scientific principles. But lately, all of Mr. Fuego's demos have gone wrong, much to the delight of Mrs. Freeze, the social studies teacher. Spills, fires, and flat balloons have left students confused and Principal Natsu worried for the students' safety. If Mr. Fuego does not get his demos under control, Principal Natsu will have no choice but to bring them to an end. Miss Caldo, the English teacher, along with two of Mr. Fuego's students, Sonny and Summer, are determined to find out what really is the matter with Mr. Fuego."-- Provided by publisher.
  Audience: Grades 4 to 6.
  ISBN 978-1-4938-1294-3 (pbk.)
  1. Science--Experiments--Juvenile literature. I. Title. II. Title: What is the matter with Mr. Fuego.
  Q164.M25 2016
  507.8--dc23
                                       2015015627

Teacher Created Materials
5301 Oceanus Drive
Huntington Beach, CA 92649-1030
http://www.tcmpub.com
ISBN 978-1-4938-1294-3
© 2016 Teacher Created Materials, Inc.
Printed in China
Nordica.072018.CA21800844

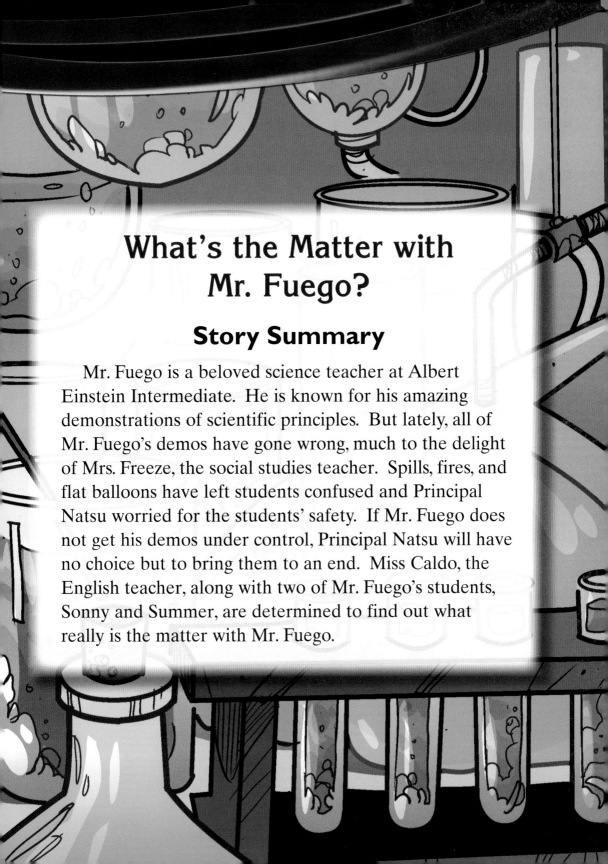

What's the Matter with Mr. Fuego?

Story Summary

Mr. Fuego is a beloved science teacher at Albert Einstein Intermediate. He is known for his amazing demonstrations of scientific principles. But lately, all of Mr. Fuego's demos have gone wrong, much to the delight of Mrs. Freeze, the social studies teacher. Spills, fires, and flat balloons have left students confused and Principal Natsu worried for the students' safety. If Mr. Fuego does not get his demos under control, Principal Natsu will have no choice but to bring them to an end. Miss Caldo, the English teacher, along with two of Mr. Fuego's students, Sonny and Summer, are determined to find out what really is the matter with Mr. Fuego.

Tips for Performing Reader's Theater

Adapted from Aaron Shepard

★ Don't let your script hide your face. If you can't see the audience, your script is too high.

★ Look up often when you speak. Don't just look at your script.

★ Talk slowly so the audience knows what you are saying.

★ Talk loudly so everyone can hear you.

★ Talk with feeling. If the character is sad, let your voice be sad. If the character is surprised, let your voice be surprised.

★ Stand up straight. Keep your hands and feet still.

★ Remember that even when you are not talking, you are still your character.

- ★ If the audience laughs, wait for them to stop before you speak again.

- ★ If someone in the audience talks, don't pay attention.

- ★ If someone walks into the room, don't pay attention.

- ★ If you make a mistake, pretend it was right.

- ★ If you drop something, try to leave it where it is until the audience is looking somewhere else.

- ★ If a reader forgets to read his or her part, see if you can read the part instead, make something up, or just skip over it. Don't whisper to the reader!

What's the Matter with Mr. Fuego?

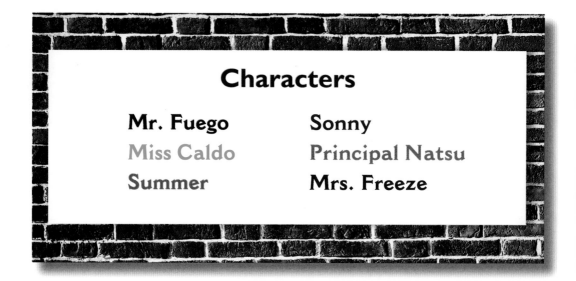

Characters

Mr. Fuego	Sonny
Miss Caldo	Principal Natsu
Summer	Mrs. Freeze

Setting

This reader's theater takes place over the span of a few days at Albert Einstein Intermediate School. Scenes occur in the hallways, Mr. Fuego's classroom, the cafeteria, and Principal Natsu's office.

Act 1

Summer:	*(shouting)* Hey, Sonny, wait up and I'll walk with you to science class!
Sonny:	Hi, Summer! How was the hockey game last night? Did you guys win?
Summer:	*(proudly)* Yes, we *girls* won. And because we won yet *again,* we remain the undefeated champions!
Sonny:	That's totally awesome! So, I just ran across Mr. Fuego in the library, and he promised he's going to show the class another new demonstration today.
Summer:	Really? I thought he might take a break from the science demonstrations since so many of them have gone wrong lately. Then again, it was pretty hilarious when the last one made our quizzes catch fire before he graded them.
Sonny:	*(laughing)* I know! Good thing it did because I was totally unprepared for that surprise quiz. Lucky for me, all my ignorance went up in brightly colored flames!

Summer: Did he figure out what went wrong with the Rainbow Flame demonstration?

Sonny: Mr. Fuego said he set up everything the previous night, and it all went perfectly during his trial run. He figures that, somehow, a different mixture of the powder chemicals must have gotten spilled onto the quizzes overnight without his knowledge, but he's completely puzzled as to how that could have come about.

Summer: How could that have happened? Mr. Fuego is usually so careful, and he always locks the door to his classroom when he leaves.

Sonny: I really don't have any idea. It's definitely very strange; but Mr. Fuego's going to show us a new demonstration today anyway, and then we're going to conduct our own experiments with our lab partners.

Summer: I wonder why he's been having so many negative results with his science demos lately. They have always been amazing in the past!

Sonny: His demonstrations are definitely a major reason why he's totally my favorite teacher.

Summer:	And, it's one of the reasons he's been awarded Teacher of the Year five years in a row.
Sonny:	Maybe he's spending too much time coaching your *undefeated* hockey team and not enough time planning his instruction.
Summer:	You're just jealous because you're an abominable ice skater.
Sonny:	I can ice-skate! I just can't body check people into walls like you obviously can.
Summer:	Do you want me to teach you? I promise I won't hurt you…too much.
Sonny:	Thanks, but no thanks. *(surprised)* Mrs. Freeze! What were you doing in Mr. Fuego's classroom?
Mrs. Freeze:	The bell hasn't rung yet; therefore, the real question is, what are you two doing standing around outside Mr. Fuego's classroom?
Summer:	We always get to Mr. Fuego's class a little early since it's our favorite class.

Mrs. Freeze:	*(mockingly)* We always get here early…it's our favorite class…blah…blah…blah. You do know that no one likes teachers' pets—especially teachers?
Sonny:	*(ignoring her comment)* Mr. Fuego is in the library checking out science experiment books if you need him, Mrs. Freeze.
Mrs. Freeze:	All I need is for you two to get out of my way so that I am not late for my own class. Tell Mr. Fuego that I borrowed some paper clips from him. Sonny, I hope you are ready for the Colonial America test because I don't light my tests on fire like other teachers.
Summer:	*(sweetly but sarcastically)* Bye, Mrs. Freeze! As always, it was lovely seeing you!
Sonny:	*(whispering)* She terrifies me.
Summer:	She terrifies everyone.
Sonny:	She left the door open. Do you think we should go inside and settle in?
Summer:	Nah, Mr. Fuego doesn't allow students in his classroom unless he's in there, remember?

Sonny & Summer: *(in unison, repeating what they have heard Mr. Fuego say many times)* "Don't take a chance. Be safe, or I'll do the dance."

Sonny: *(laughing)* I hate that safety dance.

Summer: Everyone does. That's why we all take safety precautions seriously in his class—so that we aren't tortured by seeing THE SAFETY DANCE!

Sonny: *(noticing Mr. Fuego walk up)* Hey, Mr. Fuego, you just missed Mrs. Freeze. She borrowed some of your paper clips.

Mr. Fuego: I didn't know I had paper clips. Come on in, Sonny and Summer.

Summer: Did you notice that Mrs. Freeze left the door open but we didn't go inside? We waited outside for you!

Mr. Fuego: Are you saying you don't want to see the safety dance?

Sonny: *(laughing)* That is precisely what we are saying, Mr. Fuego!

Act 2

(After the first bell of the school day)

Miss Caldo: Excuse me, Mr. Fuego?

Mr. Fuego: Well hello, Miss Caldo. What can I do for you?

Miss Caldo: My class is in the library working on outlines for their *Phantom Tollbooth* book reports, so do you mind if I stay and observe your class this morning? I love watching your demonstrations, and I learn so much from your students—especially Sonny and Summer.

Mr. Fuego: I don't mind in the least. Let me clean off my desk a bit and you can sit here.

Miss Caldo: Thank you so much.

Summer: Miss Caldo, you should have seen Mr. Fuego's last demonstration because it totally reminded me of a scene from *The Phantom Tollbooth*.

Sonny: Miss Caldo, it really did. It was just like the scene in which Milo attempts to conduct the sunrise and makes a mess of colors!

Miss Caldo:	Is that right?
Summer:	You see, Mr. Fuego was teaching us about atoms and energy…
Sonny:	…and he was telling us how astronomers figure out the distances to stars...
Summer:	…and why there are different colors in fireworks!
Sonny:	Mr. Fuego lit a bunch of different powdered chemicals in a row and it made a rainbow of fire. It was so awesome!
Summer:	But then, the rainbow of fire spread to our quizzes, and there was a crazy, gigantic mess of colors!
Miss Caldo:	*(anxiously)* Oh, my!
Sonny:	Oh, don't worry—Mr. Fuego quickly put out the fire with a fire extinguisher.
Miss Caldo:	Thank goodness! I'm glad no one was hurt, including Mr. Fuego.
Summer:	He's always extremely careful.
Miss Caldo:	Yes, I have heard something about a "safety dance."

Sonny: No! Don't even mention it! Trust me, it isn't something you want to see.

Summer: Yeah, it's bad, *really bad*. I mean, it's atrocious.

Miss Caldo: *(laughs)* I'm impressed that you're using your new vocabulary words, Summer.

Act 3

(After the second bell of the school day)

Mr. Fuego: Everyone, please be seated so that I can begin class. I have a quick demonstration, after which you will be conducting your own experiments with your lab partners. Pay close attention, as befits a quality scientist. Miss Caldo, since you will be joining us today, would you be so kind as to assist me here at the front of the class?

Miss Caldo: Sure. What do you need me to do?

Mr. Fuego: Do you know what everything—and I mean *everything*—is made of?

Miss Caldo: I'm sorry, I'm not following you.

Mr. Fuego:	What do you mean? What's the *matter*?
Miss Caldo:	Nothing's the matter, it's just that I don't understand the quest…oh, wait! I get it. *Matter*! Everything is made of matter!
Mr. Fuego:	Exactly! Today we are going to learn about three states of matter: solid, liquid, and gas. Miss Caldo, can you suggest an example of each one of these three types of matter?
Miss Caldo:	Well, a solid could be this chemistry notebook, a liquid could be the vinegar in that bottle you have there, and a gas could be the air in your lungs that you'll use to inflate the balloon you're holding.
Mr. Fuego:	Well done, Miss Caldo. Now, you may think I'm going to blow air into this balloon to inflate it, but I'm not. I'm going to create a gas called *carbon dioxide*, using both a solid and a liquid.
Miss Caldo:	Should I go sit down? Is it safe for me to be standing here?
Mr. Fuego:	*(laughing)* Yes, Miss Caldo, it is safe; however, you may take a seat. Thank you for your assistance—and class, give Miss Caldo a round of applause.

Miss Caldo: Thank you, thank you!

Mr. Fuego: I'm going to put the liquid—vinegar—into this plastic water bottle. Next, I'm going to put a solid—baking soda—into this balloon, and finally, I'm going to wrap the mouth of the balloon around the top of the water bottle. The baking soda will drop into the bottle, and *voilà*!

Sonny: Umm, is something supposed to happen?

Summer: The solid should have mixed with the liquid to create a gas that would blow up the balloon!

Mr. Fuego: Yes, Summer, exactly…but I don't know why it didn't work. *(sniffing)* Wait, this isn't vinegar! This is water! Someone must have switched out the vinegar with water.

Miss Caldo: That is so strange. Who would do that?

Mr. Fuego: Well it doesn't *matter* because it's time for you to begin your own lab experiments. Everyone meet with your lab partners and put on your safety gear.

Act 4

Principal Natsu: Mr. Fuego, do you mind if I eat lunch with you?

Mr. Fuego: Not at all, Principal Natsu—please have a seat.

Principal Natsu: I heard another one of your demonstrations failed miserably today.

Mr. Fuego: Unfortunately, yes, but no one was hurt and I know exactly what went wrong. Someone switched my vinegar with water. Strange, right?

Principal Natsu: Yes, strange indeed. However, I'm enormously concerned about the safety of the students at this intermediate school, Mr. Fuego, as I'm sure you can easily understand.

Mr. Fuego: I assure you, Principal Natsu, that my students have never been in danger and that the safety of my students is always my number-one priority.

Principal Natsu: I believe you, Mr. Fuego; however, if this happens on another occasion I will be forced to terminate all scientific demonstrations in your classroom.

Mr. Fuego: I understand, Principal Natsu, but I promise you it will not happen again.

Miss Caldo: I'm sorry to interrupt your conversation, gentlemen, but a package has arrived in the front office for you, Mr. Fuego.

Mr. Fuego: Oh, thank you, Miss Caldo! That must be my baby diapers.

Caldo & Natsu: *(in unison)* Baby diapers?!

Miss Caldo: But Mr. Fuego, you do not have a baby. You don't have any children.

Mr. Fuego: *(laughing)* That is correct, but I needed sodium polyacrylate. I saw a coupon online for a pack of baby diapers, and the coupon—combined with a free shipping code I had—made it less expensive to purchase a small pack of diapers online than to order the sodium polyacrylate alone.

Principal Natsu: What possible connection could the chemical sodium polyacrylate have with diapers for infants?

Mr. Fuego: It's the super-absorbent polymer used in baby diapers. I'm going to pull the diapers apart and sift out the sodium polyacrylate to use in my next demonstration.

Principal Natsu: Well, please be careful with this demo—even excessively careful. I don't want it to be your last, nor, I'm sure, do you. Your enjoyable and surprising demonstrations have become famous with the students, and they adore them. I don't want to be the villain who must bring them to an end. Now, if you will both excuse me, I have a meeting with the superintendent.

Miss Caldo: Goodbye, Principal Natsu. Mr. Fuego, do you think perhaps someone is sabotaging your demonstrations? Is there anyone who is upset with you, or perhaps jealous? I mean, you have won the coveted Teacher of the Year award five years in a row, and perhaps someone is envious of that.

Mr. Fuego: *(laughing)* Miss Caldo, I'm sure there is a logical explanation for all this, so there is no need to concern yourself with any crazy conspiracy theories. Now, if you will excuse me, I have to go pull apart some baby diapers for tomorrow's demonstration.

Act 5

Mrs. Freeze:	*(shouting)* Tai! Tai! Excuse me! Hello! I need to speak with you! It's incredibly urgent and very important.
Principal Natsu:	Mrs. Freeze, I would prefer that you call me Principal Natsu, and please do not gallivant down the hallways shouting at the top of your lungs. I would prefer that my teachers follow the same rules, guidelines, and decorum that the students are expected to follow.
Mrs. Freeze:	*(mockingly)* Follow the rules…blah, blah, blah. I really don't have time for one of your tedious and pointless lectures right now. I need you to stop Mr. Fuego from performing yet another one of his failed demonstrations.
Principal Natsu:	What are you talking about, Mrs. Freeze?
Mrs. Freeze:	That ridiculous teacher is about to do another one of his ridiculous demos! Are you not aware that all his demonstrations lately have been huge failures? He's been lucky that no one has gotten hurt, but who's to say his next demo won't burn the school down!

Principal Natsu: Mrs. Freeze, I am well aware of the problems Mr. Fuego has been having with his demonstrations, but I assure you that safety in his classroom is his top priority. Today he is conducting a demo with sodium polyacrylate, which he explained to me and now has my approval.

Mrs. Freeze: *(angrily)* Well that is ridiculous! He messes up again and again and no one cares! He puts the students in danger and you don't do anything about it. I'm appalled, Principal Natsu, simply appalled. This man is a menace to our school, and yet you stand idly by and do nothing! NOTHING!

Principal Natsu: I have had a talk with Mr. Fuego, and he knows that if this demonstration goes wrong today, it will be his last. I am on top of the situation. In fact, I am observing his class today.

Mrs. Freeze: Wonderful! Fabulous! That is great news! Now you will finally get to see him fail with your own eyes. This will be excellent.

Principal Natsu: Why are you so sure that Mr. Fuego's demonstration will fail, Mrs. Freeze?

Mrs. Freeze: Well, umm, you know it's just that he's had so many failures as of late, so I'm sure that today will be no different. I mean, he got the chemicals he's using from baby diapers!

Principal Natsu: How did you know that?

Mrs. Freeze: You told me.

Principal Natsu: No, I most certainly did not. All I said was that he was conducting a demonstration with sodium polyacrylate.

Mrs. Freeze: Exactly…and sodium polyacrylate is used in diapers, so I just put two and two together.

Principal Natsu: You know that sodium polyacrylate is used in baby diapers? I didn't think that would be common knowledge for a social studies teacher.

Mrs. Freeze: Well it's common knowledge for *this* social studies teacher. If you must know, I am quite well-rounded and well-informed, Principal Natsu. Now if you will excuse me, I have a lecture to give on the Boston Tea Party. Have a wonderful time in Mr. Fuego's class. I wouldn't sit in the front row if I were you!

Principal Natsu:	Goodbye, Mrs. Freeze. Have a good day.
Miss Caldo:	Principal Natsu, do you have a second?
Principal Natsu:	Yes, Miss Caldo. How can I help you?
Miss Caldo:	Could we meet briefly after school today? I have something important I would like to discuss with you.
Principal Natsu:	Yes, I will be in my office at three o'clock. Is everything all right, Miss Caldo?
Miss Caldo:	Yes, but I would like to discuss a few things I've noticed regarding Mr. Fuego and Mrs. Freeze.
Principal Natsu:	Those two could not be more different if they tried, could they? I look forward to hearing what you have to say, Miss Caldo. I will see you after school.
Miss Caldo:	Thank you, Principal Natsu. See you then!

Poem: Fire and Ice

Act 6

Mr. Fuego: This is simply water I turned green with food coloring. I'm going to pour it into this beaker and it will magically turn into a solid. Here we go! Now, I turn the beaker upside down and *voilà*, it's a sol...oh, no!

Sonny: Mr. Fuego! Move your cell phone quick! The green water is going to get it!

Summer: What happened, Mr. Fuego?

Principal Natsu: Yes, Mr. Fuego! What happened *this* time?

Mr. Fuego: I'm not sure. The sodium polyacrylate powder I extracted from the baby diapers was in the bottom of this beaker. It should have mixed with the water to quickly make a solid...

Summer: ...so that when you turned the beaker upside down nothing would have spilled because it changed from one state of matter to another.

Sonny: Something must be wrong with the powder, Mr. Fuego!

Principal Natsu: Maybe you should not have extracted it from baby diapers? I expect to see you in my office after hockey practice, Mr. Fuego.

Act 7

Principal Natsu: We'll have to make this quick, Miss Caldo. I'm meeting with Mr. Fuego shortly.

Miss Caldo: I'll get straight to the point then, Principal Natsu. I believe Mrs. Freeze is sabotaging Mr. Fuego's science demonstrations.

Principal Natsu: What evidence do you have to support this wild claim of yours, Miss Caldo?

Miss Caldo: Well, I've been doing some investigative work. Did you know Mrs. Freeze has been in and out of Mr. Fuego's classroom over the last several weeks? I saw her exiting his classroom just last night as I was packing up to leave. I knew Mr. Fuego was coaching hockey practice, so I stopped and inquired what she was doing. She barked at me for inquiring about her suspicious behavior and then told me dismissively that she was borrowing paper clips.

Principal Natsu: I am afraid that is simply not enough evidence Miss Caldo.

Miss Caldo: I figured you would say that, so I started casually asking some students if they have noticed anything unusual. Sonny and Summer mentioned that they, too, saw Mrs. Freeze leaving Mr. Fuego's classroom yesterday before the first bell rang. When they asked what she was doing, she coldly snapped that she was just borrowing *paper clips*. Who could possibly need that many paper clips, Principal Natsu?

Principal Natsu: That *is* suspicious behavior. Truthfully, I spoke with her today and she knew that Mr. Fuego's demonstration involved baby diapers. I thought it was odd. I'll speak with her right now.

Sonny & Summer: *(in unison, shouting)* Principal Natsu! Principal Natsu! It's Mrs. Freeze!

Principal Natsu: Calm down. One at a time—Summer, why are you not at hockey practice?

Summer:	I had to skip it to prove that Mr. Fuego is innocent. It's not his fault his demonstrations keep getting messed up because Mrs. Freeze is behind everything!
Sonny:	Yeah! Mr. Fuego's powder wasn't the right stuff. It was switched with baby powder! He said so himself. And the other day someone switched his vinegar with water!
Summer:	And before that, someone had spilled an assortment of powders all over our quizzes so that they would catch fire!
Principal Natsu:	What makes you two think Mrs. Freeze was responsible for these actions?
Summer:	We just overheard her bragging about it on her cell phone in the hallway!
Sonny:	Yeah, she said she was tired of his demonstrations and didn't want him to win Teacher of the Year again, and that it was *her* turn to win now.
Summer:	Yeah, like that's ever going to happen when all she ever does is lecture, lecture, lecture and give mega-heaps of busy work.

Sonny:
Totally! She's like the Terrible Trivium in *The Phantom Tollbooth,* Miss Caldo.

Miss Caldo:
I'm glad you like the book, Sonny, but let's not go there right now.

Principal Natsu:
All right, everyone out of my office. I'm going to speak with Mrs. Freeze.

Mrs. Freeze:
Mr. Fuego, I apologize for sabotaging your demonstrations. I never meant to get you into trouble. I was just jealous of your popularity with the students and of all your Teacher of the Year awards. I think you are a fine teacher, and I hope one day to be as well liked as you.

Mr. Fuego:
Thank you for your honesty, Mrs. Freeze. If you would like, I could help you with some of your lessons. For instance, have you ever thought of reenacting the Boston Tea Party with your students? I think the school pool would make a great Boston Harbor.

Mrs. Freeze: Well, there's an idea! So, what is your next demonstration? Don't worry, I promise not to switch out any of your materials.

Mr. Fuego: Well, we are still studying matter, so I'm going to show my students how something can be simultaneously a solid and a liquid, using a subwoofer and the lyrics to "Jingle Bells." Intrigued, Mrs. Freeze?

Mrs. Freeze: Huh?

Mr. Fuego: You should stop by and see it for yourself.

Mrs. Freeze: I think I will!

Song: Jingle Bells

Fire and Ice

by Robert Frost

Some say the world will end in fire,
Some say in ice.
From what I've tasted of desire
I hold with those who favor fire.
But if it had to perish twice,
I think I know enough of hate
To say that for destruction ice
Is also great
And would suffice.

Jingle Bells

by James Pierpont

Dashing through the snow
In a one-horse open sleigh,
O'er the fields we go
Laughing all the way.
Bells on bobtail ring
Making spirits bright.
What fun it is to ride and sing
A sleighing song tonight!

Jingle bells, jingle bells,
Jingle all the way;
Oh! what fun it is to ride
In a one-horse open sleigh.
Jingle bells, jingle bells,
Jingle all the way;
Oh! what fun it is to ride
In a one-horse open sleigh.

This is an abridged version of the original song.

Glossary

absorbent—able to take in and hold liquid

beaker—a wide glass with a lip for pouring that is used in chemistry to measure and hold liquids

carbon dioxide—a colorless gas produced when people breathe out

conspiracy theories—theories that explain situations as being the result of a secret plot

gas—a substance such as air that has no fixed shape

liquid—a substance such as water that is able to flow freely

matter—the thing that everything is made of and takes up space

polymer—a chemical compound made of small molecules that are arranged to form a larger molecule

sabotaging—damaging or destroying something on purpose so that it does not work correctly

sodium polyacrylate—a chemical polymer that is super absorbent and used in household items such as diapers

solid—not having the form of a gas nor liquid